To:

From:

Love Letters

Arnold Adoff
illustrated by Lisa Desimini

SCHOLASTIC INC.
New York Toronto London Auckland Sydney

This book was originally published in hardcover by the Blue Sky Press in 1997.

Special thanks to Hasbro, Inc. for the use of MR. POTATO HEAD®.
MR. POTATO HEAD® is a trademark of Hasbro, Inc.
All rights reserved.

ISBN 0-590-48479-6

12 11 10 9 8 7 6 5 4 3 2 1   1   8 9/9 0 1 2 3/0

Printed in the U.S.A.   14

Original Blue Sky Press edition designed by Kristina Iulo

Dear Ginger Belle:
These Love Letters,
These Love Poems
Are
For
You
For All The D a y s
Of All The Y e a r s.

Y o u r O w n A r n.

For Matt
L.D.

Dear Ms. Back Row:

I t h i n k
I like you
    a   lot, especially
            since
           Christmas
when you wore that angel
crown on top of your so
f l u f f y brown h a i r.
Just
smile
at me
o n e
t i m e
on your way past my desk.

Yours: First Seat First Row.

Gg Hh Ii Jj Kk

Dear New Boy:

at   the
blackboard
just
arrived in
town with
        all
        the
        answers.
Can you see
that
one
plus
one equals
the
sum of you
and   who?

Your Only Correct Answer:
        Only Me.

Dear Playground Snow Girl:

I'll love you until
my nose falls off,
              until
my toes freeze
              inside
              my
              sneaks,
              until
m y m o u t h
goes s o u t h in
              the
              winter wind.
I'm waving
my fingers
              inside
              warm
              mittens.   Please
              wave
              back.

Your Frozen Friend:
Frosty The Snow Boy.

Dear Playground Snow Boy:

Sorry you are frosty
frozen.
Now
watch my hand wave
you
far
a w a y
from me
and my playing friends.
M a y b e
t o m o r r o w.
M a y b e not.
I love to run
when it's hot
or cold,
but I always
run
a l o n e.

Your Not-Yet Friend:
I c i c l e E y e s.

Dear Teacher:

I
hope
you never
find out
this red
h e a r t
is
from me.
I
like
to   stay
q u i e t
in
the
    c l a s s
    crowd.

Yours As A Mouse.

Dear Mrs. Nicely:

I love you more than peanut butters, more than chocolate chips. I love you more than Elmer Fuddy stutters, more than Shamu flips. flips. flips.

Your Secret Student.

Dear
Mrs.
McNasty:

I
almost
like
you
today.

Your
Valentine
Avenger.

Dear Slick:

I love my
mom ma and my pop pa,
         and my gerbils,
         and
         one hamster,
and
my good dog,
and macaroni and cheese,
and my mountain trail
                 bike.
But
I'd leave them all
to shoot baskets
with you on even
the coldest
after
school
afternoon.

Yours: The Dribbler.

Dear Tall Girl At Front Table:

I love you more than peanut butter cookies
                                    crumble.
I love you more than yellow b e e s bumble.
I also you more than dark thunder c l o u d s
  love
                                    r u m b l e.
I especially
  love
        you more than
me

m u m b l i n g

e x c u s e

me

after

I stumbled all over you   itwasanaccident.
as I walked up to get help
on Tuesday's math problem.

Your Future Friend: Big Foot.

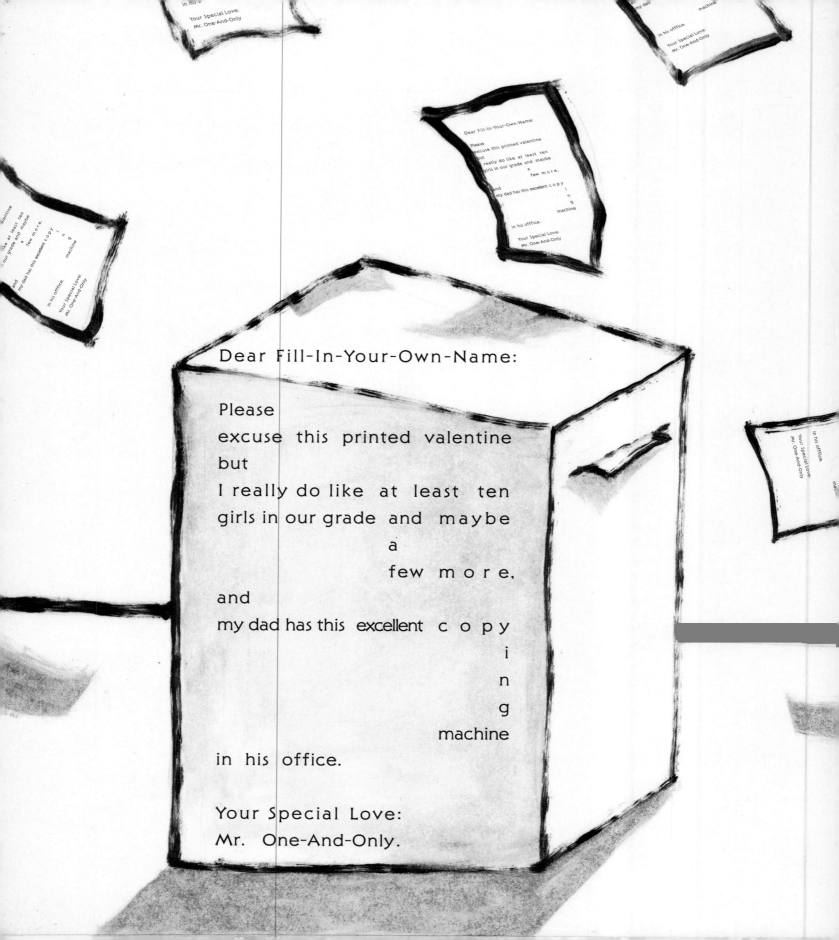

Dear Fill-In-Your-Own-Name:

Please
excuse this printed valentine
but
I really do like at least ten
girls in our grade and maybe
a
few more,
and
my dad has this excellent c o p y
i
n
g
machine

in his office.

Your Special Love:
Mr. One-And-Only.

Dear Gram:

I
very
much
love
your sugar cookies
and chocolate fudge.
B u t
I am
even
f u l l of love
when all your
j a r s
a r e e m p t y.

Your Grandson: Big Belly.

Dear Mom:

First: K e e p   m o m m i n g.
Second:
            I'm really thanking you.
Third: I'm s e r i o u s.
Fourth:
            Don't laugh.
Fifth: Please kiss
                      only
                        on
                         the
            c h e e k.

Your Big Son: The Kid Himself.

Dear Hard Working Dad:

Even when you snore
on the couch, I am
proud
with
a
full
heart for
you.

Your Son With Earplugs.

Dear Little Sis:

Here is a lesson for you:
   even though   these
            scissors
are supposed to be for
        u
         s
       kids,
I did cut my finger
on the sharp edges
cutting out this heart
       f o r
      you.
P.S. #1:
Please
notice: the two drops
    ofmyblood,   y
                        u
                        c
next to your name   h,
on the front of this
        card.
P.S. #2:
The messy white paste-looking lumps
are only lumps of messy white paste.

Your Big Broth.

Dear Older Brother:

My list of reasons:

1. You were here first.
2. You will always be older than me.
3. I love you when
      you listen
      and don't
        h i t.

Your B e s t Brother: Peace.

Dear
Self:

How
are
you?
How
am
I?
I
am
fine.
Fine
I
am: because
I
am
my number
one
valentine.

Your
First
Love.

Dear Old Cat:

Under
the
bed:
your tail
s w i n g s
s o
s l o w l y
this
Monday
morning
before
s c h o o l.
We'll play
       this
afternoon.

Your Sleepy Head Girl.

Dear
Dog
Spot:

I
love
you
this
special
day
and
for
ever.

Your Best Play Pal:
The Biscuit Girl.

Dear Prince:

My hair is very short,
I don't live high up
at the top of s o m e
                c a s t l e,
and I don't
n e e d the
r e s c u e.
J u s t
ride
your
blue
bike
down m y
street   and ring the bell
         this S a t u r d a y.

We can
chase
those
dragons
to
gether.

Your Potential Princess.

Dear Once Upon A Time:

I
k n o w
we can
write
that
story
together
i f
we
just
put
our
heads:
ear
t o
ear,
our
faces:
eye
t o
eye.

Your Happy Ending.